The Trouble
with Oatmeal

Story by Janet Slater Bottin

Illustrations by
Pat Reynolds and Rae Dale

Contents

Chapter 1

The Trouble with Jess

Jess and I have been best friends for as long as I can remember.

She always used to say, "Lucy, you're my best friend. You never make fun of me, and I can tell you anything."

Kids used to make fun of Jess because her last name is Tree. "Hey, Tree," they'd say, "where are your leaves?"

Jess would always answer, "I'm deciduous!"

Most of them didn't even know what deciduous meant. Then Jess would say, "Watch out! It's contagious!"

Because of that joke about "leaves," I didn't understand at first what Jess was saying when we set out for school together a few months ago.

She said, "Lucy, there's something I have to tell you ... I'm going to leave."

Jess's being funny, I thought ... Am I supposed to laugh? But Jess wasn't smiling.

She explained that her mom had gotten a new job in Steepleton and they would be leaving in two weeks.

"I don't want to leave you, Lucy. I hated it when my Dad went away. I HATE people leaving! And I HATE leaving people!"

We threw our arms around each other and cried ...

Chapter 2

A Great Idea

The next two weeks went past too fast.

I dreaded saying good-bye to Jess. We'd lived next door to each other and played together all our lives. We'd always sat together at school, and we'd shared everything—even her cat and my little brother.

My brother, Brady, loves Jess's cat, Oatmeal, and I knew he would miss Oatmeal as much as I was going to miss Jess.

After the moving van left, Jess and her mom crammed the rest of their belongings, including Oatmeal, into their car and came to say good-bye.

Just as Jess was about to squeeze herself into the car, Mom handed her a big pad of writing paper and a bundle of envelopes, already stamped. And guess what—all the envelopes were addressed to me!

I waved until their car was a faraway speck. I felt as empty inside as the house next door.

Then Mom handed *me* a big writing pad and a bundle of envelopes, which were already stamped and addressed to Jess's new address.

I said, "Thanks, Mom. Great idea!" and ran inside to start my first letter to Jess.

Chapter 3

A Quiz

Dear Jess,

Guess what? I got a 'good-bye' present too, just like yours. We can use our good-bye presents to say 'hello' to each other!

By the time this letter arrives you'll be in your new house. Answer these questions correctly and you might win a prize!!!

1. What is your house like?

2. What is your bedroom like?

3. What are your neighbors like?

4. How is Oatmeal? Was she carsick on the way there?

5. Were you?

6. When do you start your new school? I hope it won't be too scary.

Write soon,
Lucy

As soon as my letter was finished, I ran to the mailbox and mailed it.

Chapter 4

The Answers

I waited a whole week for Jess's letter ...

Dear Lucy,

    I was so happy when your letter came. I wanted to write back right away, but we've been so busy unpacking.

    Here are your answers!!!

    1. Our home is an apartment in a high-rise building. It's okay, but there's no yard. There's a park nearby, but Mom won't let me play there alone.

2. My bedroom's not bad, now that I've put up my posters.

3. Our neighbors seem friendly — but there are no kids.

4. Oatmeal is acting strangely, so we've had to keep her locked inside. Mom put butter on her paws — that's supposed to help her settle into her new home. No, she wasn't carsick.

5. As IF!!! (Even if I were, would I tell anyone? Would YOU?)

6. I start school on Monday. I'm scared stiff!

Okay, so — where's my prize?

miss U! Write again SOON,

Jess

Chapter 5

The Trouble with Brady

Dear Jess,

    It was so good to get your letter. Here's your prize!

I hope your new school's working out, and the kids aren't being pains about your name.

I'm still sitting by an empty space at school, but somebody's started moving into your old house. I've heard kids' voices, but I haven't seen any kids yet.

Brady can't understand where you and Oatmeal have gone. He keeps staring at your old house through the hedge and calling "Sess!" and "Oatmeeel!"

He's starting preschool on Monday, so that should keep him busy.

Is Oatmeal settled in yet?

Here's something to keep your brains from going rusty.

Help—I've just seen a kid next door!

It's A BOY!!!

I miss U, 2!!!!

Lucy

Chapter 6

The Trouble with Oatmeal

Dear Lucy,

Thanks for the stickers! I showed them to Billie and told her all about you. She thinks you sound cool—she wants to meet you.

Billie lives two floors down with her dad. I met her yesterday when she nearly ran over me in her wheelchair! She speeds around in it like a race car driver. And she laughs at my jokes like you used to do.

Oatmeal is still behaving strangely. All day she prowls and meows around the apartment, as if she's lost something. And she climbs up on the windowsill and stares out the window. We have to watch that she doesn't slip out through the door when we go in and out. Mom said if Oatmeal got lost in Steepleton, we'd probably never find her.

School isn't nearly as bad as I thought it would be.

Anyway, how old is THAT BOY, and have you seen any other kids next door?

👁 miss U more!
Jess

Chapter 7

All Sorts

Dear Jess,

Billie sounds nice. I'd like to meet her too, and I wish I could see YOU ...

About Oatmeal: Dad said she might be freaked out about leaving her old place. What he actually said was: "She could be traumatized about being moved from her familiar surroundings."

PARENTS!!

He also said she could be homesick.

I've met THAT BOY next door. He's not bad—for a boy! His name is Jack. He's nine, too, and in my class, and guess whose empty space he's filling?

He'll never make up for YOU—but he's better than nothing. Actually, he's quite funny. I've been getting into nearly as much trouble for giggling in class as I did when YOU sat beside me!

Jack has a thirteen-year-old sister named Sarah. He says she's "a pain with pimples."

Brady likes preschool, and he looks so cute with his mini backpack. But he still keeps calling for Oatmeal.

I miss U most !!!
Lucy

Chapter 8

Oatmeal and Brady

Dear Lucy,

I got your letter. But this is just a quick note to tell you the AWFUL news. Oatmeal IS MISSING!

She escaped yesterday as Mom was coming in the front door. We called her and chased her, but she just ran faster! We searched the neighborhood for hours, calling her and asking people if they'd seen her ...

We're putting "lost cat" flyers in people's mailboxes. I'm REALLY WORRIED, Lucy. The streets here are jammed with traffic.

LOST
Where is
Oatmeal the Cat?
If you have seen her call
5 5 5 - 4 6 3 0
We miss her !

Dear Jess,

How AWFUL! Poor Oatmeal ... Poor you!

I do hope she'll be found by the time you get this letter. I know just how losing someone feels, because this afternoon Brady was missing from preschool!

Somehow he got past the high fence and the special lock on the gate. The teacher wondered if he'd slipped out the gate with a group of children visiting from another preschool. So she phoned that preschool, but no one had seen Brady. Then she phoned the police. It was all so dreadful ...

When the police officer arrived, we all started searching for Brady. Mom and I went down one side of the street, looking and asking in all the stores. The police officer went down the other side. No one had seen Brady.

Then the lady who owns 'Field's Furniture' remembered that a small boy had been playing with her cat in the store doorway.

THAT sounded like Brady! Mom and I looked around inside the store, and *there he was*—curled up on a sofa with the cat, fast asleep!

WHEW—were we glad to see him!!!

Send me news of Oatmeal, SOON,

Lucy

Chapter 9

Two Surprises

Dear Lucy,

I'm very glad that Brady's found
He's really nice 2 B around
I'm every bit as glad as U
I love him like a brother 2.

Oh where, oh where
has my little cat gone?
Oh where, oh where can she be?
With her soft, gray fur
And her happy purr
Oh where, oh where is she?

28

Dear Jess,

It was fantastic hearing your voice last night! Wasn't that just THE BEST NEWS?

When Dad said, "Such good news is worth a long-distance call," I couldn't get to the phone fast enough!

Like I told you, I couldn't believe my eyes when I saw Brady playing outside with Oatmeal! She seemed as happy to see us as we were to see her. I can't get over how fat she looks, after such a long trip. Maybe she hitchhiked! Jess, it was so GREAT of you to say you'd rather let Brady have Oatmeal than risk her running away again.

You should see the two of them together! I WISH you could.

My turn for a prize!!!

Love, Lucy

In the mail today I got this!

To Lucy

YOU'RE INVITED! I'M EXCITED!
Here's the latest! It's THE GREATEST!
School break is just six weeks away
And Mom said YOU can come and stay!
We'll play a lot and talk a heap
(And maybe, if there's time, we'll sleep)
Ask your parents if you can stay
Please let me know real quick, OK?
P.S. Billie can't wait to meet you as well.
You've just got to come!

Mom and Dad said "YES"!

Chapter 10

Five More Surprises

I'd had two happy surprises already that week. I had no idea there'd be more!

On Saturday morning, Brady grabbed my hand and dragged me to the linen closet. Oatmeal was lying there, and Brady was pointing and saying, "Look, Lucy—little Oatmeals!"

Then I saw something wriggle— something small and gray. I looked closer. I thought ... I *don't* believe this! Oatmeal has had kittens! FIVE kittens!

That happened six weeks ago. Three of the kittens have just gone to new homes—Jack has one. Guess who are getting the other two!